The Fragrance of Nature and Love

Manoj Krishnan

The Fragrance of Nature and Love

An
Anthology of Poems

By
Manoj Krishnan

Kalamos Literary Services LLP

Kalamos Literary Services LLP
Email: info@kalamos.co.in | editorial@kalamos.co.in

Published in 2017
by
Kalamos Literary Services
ISBN- 978-81-935033-3-1

Typeset & Cover Designed at Kalamos Literary Services LLP

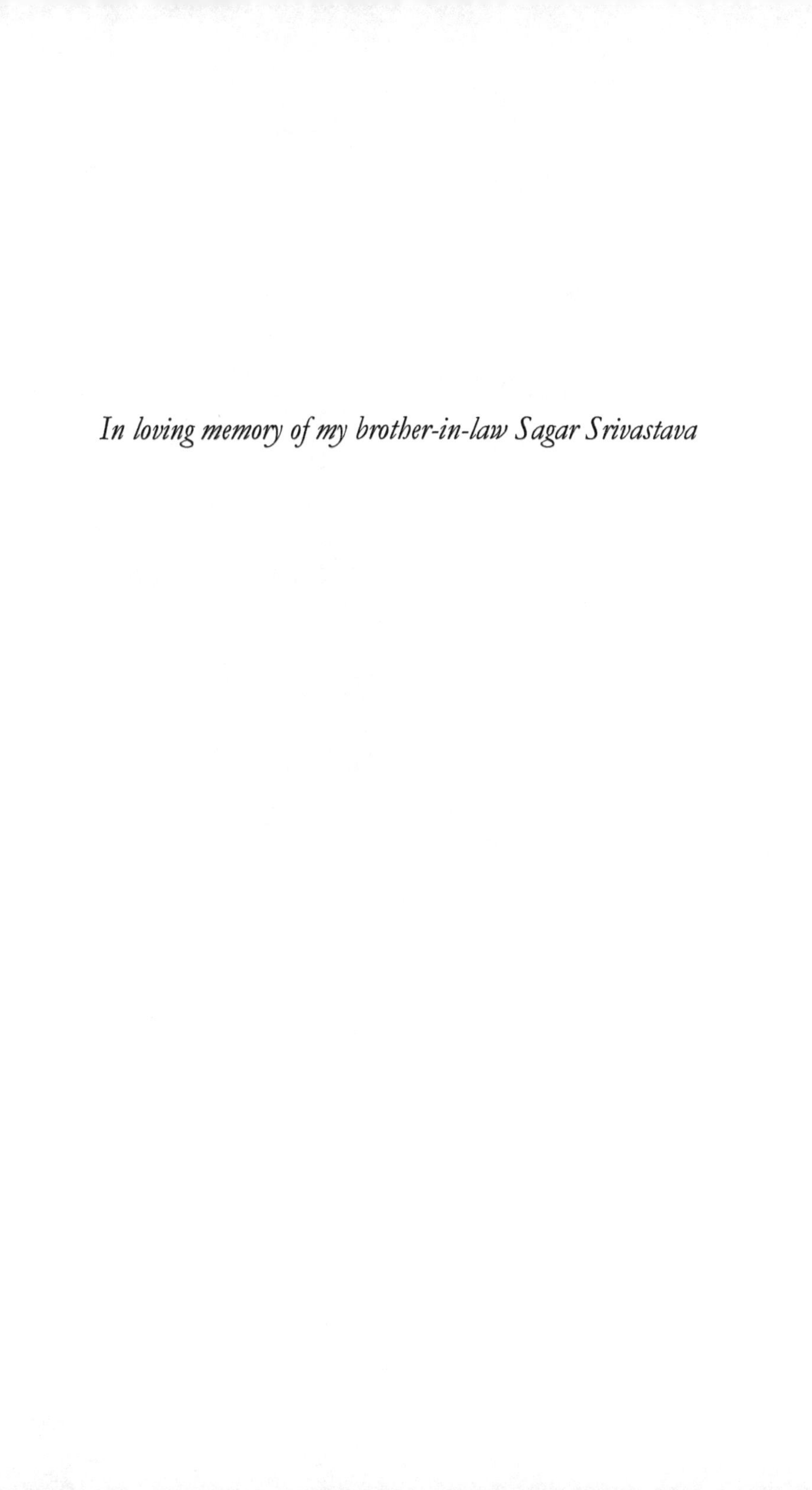

In loving memory of my brother-in-law Sagar Srivastava

INDEX

ACKNOWLEDGEMENT

First and foremost, I would like to thank Almighty for giving me the power to believe in myself and pursue my dreams.

Heartfelt gratitude to Kalamos Literary Services, Anuj Kumar and Sana Shekh for being so kind and helpful during this memorable journey.

I'm eternally grateful to my mother for her support and blessing. Thanks, Mom, to be with me throughout this journey.

Special thanks to my extraordinary wife, Shivpriya Srivastava for her patience and unconditional love.

My heart goes to my nephew, Neelkanth Chandramauli who reviews my literary compositions and gives his honest opinion. Thank you, dear!

Humble gratitude to Bina Pillai ma'am for taking time out of her busy schedule to pen a foreword for this Anthology.

Last but not the least, I'm grateful to my entire family and friends for their perennial support.

FOREWORD

Manoj Krishnan's Anthology "The fragrance of nature and love," is a collection of his prize-winning poems which have won top honors in national and international literary contests. It's different because his poems have profound underlying messages and the emphasis is on life, love, and positivity. It inspires you to live your life well and move on however arduous the journey might be.

The readers can relate to these poems easily. The poems flow smoothly as the rhythm is maintained and the poems are broken into beautiful stanzas. The presentation is eye-catching. There is a logical progression of thoughts and ideas. The descriptions are wonderful that you are carried off very easily into his world of poetry. He has used the metaphors and similes brilliantly that one can understand the more profound concepts, just the way he has conceived. It is easy to get addicted to his poems.

These beautifully written poems have the aesthetic capacity and capability to evoke different emotions, feelings, and sentiments in the minds of the readers.

A nice mix of poems about different themes that makes it an interesting read, you will not want to keep the book down once you begin.

The cover of the book and the title is perfect; his poems blend with it. Overall, I loved his collection of poems for the lyrics and the flowery language which comes directly from his heart. It is difficult for me to say which one is my favorite because I like all his poems for different reasons. But these two poems stand out. In the poem "Beauty and the Knight" the last four lines leaves an impact and touches the chord of your heart.

"Contemplating what will happen with him,
When she would leave before the morning;
Perhaps then his heart beats would stop,

From his inconsolable eyes, tears will drop."

In "Pleasure is a treasure beyond measure" the lines below are profound.

"All are in blind race to gather worldly medallions;

Despite the knowledge, they are in oblivion.

But one day when they would get tired in this race;

They'll repent for being trapped in the elusive maze.

Possibly destiny may give them another chance;

But the time missed may never come again."

His poems charge our imagination; leaving us with a want to read more. That is the power of his narrative. The emotions and passion of the poet are reflecting in Manoj Krishnan's work. I wish him all the best and welcome him to the realms of poetry, knowing that he will be riding high.

-Bina Pillai

An Explorer, writer, and crusader for peace and social issues.

Passionate about Life, Love, and Nature

Author of "Lyrical Rhythms Of My Heart"

Email id: bhina23@hotmail.com

INTRODUCTION

People often ask me how did I become a poet? I also don't know the exact answer. But since childhood, I've been weaving couplets and stories in my thoughts. I started writing English poetry one year ago. My entry in the world of English poetry was just a coincidence. One day, I received the friend request of an eminent poet in the social media platform. I accepted it and started reading her award-winning poems. Soon I became interested in participating in the poetry contests. It was pleasant surprise to see myself winning top honors in national and international literary competitions. I felt blessed to be chosen as the winner by the jury panel of eminent literary luminaries from all over the globe. Then one day I thought to compile them into a poetry book and share my poems to all my readers.

This anthology contains my seventy-five winning poems. I hope readers would like this bouquet of poems. May Almighty help us to spread the fragrance of nature and love all over the world.

Manoj Krishnan
Author

1
Solitary Peacock

Far away from the chaos of the world
Amid the lush green woods unfurled,
Missing scream of the fellow creature,
Resting in recluse in the lap of nature,
Where all pretend to be a lame duck,
Finding a true companion is also luck.
In pensive mood and desolate state,
Solitary peacock awaits his soul mate.

Attainment is illusion on this long trail;
Separation is a reality in the mortal tale.
In the meretricious glitter of this world,
Portrait of relationship is always blurred.
Life is fair with opulence in abundance,
Still, we search for love amid hundreds.
Dreaming of dance in the drizzling rain,
Solitary peacock waits for his soul mate.

In the mundane world of subtle realism,
Contemplative solitude has a mysticism.
Loneliness haunts but serenity soothes;
It depends on what we prefer to choose.
In this life where all fight for existence,
A friend can shorten the long distance.
Beyond analytical mind's all cognizance,
Solitary peacock waits for his soul mate.

2
Motherhood

Resting on the yellow velvet of nature,
I am cherishing this beautiful picture.
A lady draped in printed yellow cloth,
Looking jovial, far from daytime sloth;
You will understand reason of her joy,
When you find her playing with a toy;
Amidst violent African neighborhood,
She basks in the glory of motherhood.

See! Little angel is wriggling in her lap,
Perhaps, she wishes to fill the only gap.
In glow of resplendent spring morning,
Her gurgling face looks very charming.
She stares at her mother with surprise,
Maybe searching herself in those eyes;
In the world where nothing seems good,
She basks in the glory of motherhood.

I am amazed at her unflinching spirit,
Is she nescient of the life she inherits?
As a mother, she knows her strength,
To save her child, can go to any length.
I salute this sacred bond of maternity,
A spirit that has traversed the eternity;
Kissing gently little princess of woods,
She basks in the glory of motherhood.

3
Rhythm of Our love

Where we can dance to the rhythm of our love;
I wish to be with you in that imaginary world.
Where I will relish the warmth of your breath;
And my fingers will play with your hairy chest.

Where you can kiss my wet eyes with passion;
And leave on my heart a profound impression.
Where my stolen heart will beat at your rhythm;
I wish to live there in the shadow of your love.

Where we are far away from taunts of the world;
And same old sarcasm, to see you with a blind girl.
In the sweet fragrance of our pure and divine love,
I can feel the symphony of our perfect rhythm.

4

Generosity of The Salmon Orange Rose

Why are you so generous O! Salmon Orange Rose?
Is there any deep secret, which you don't disclose?
The aromatic fragrance you spread in this nature;
Is one aspect of your generosity for all creatures.

Sparkling dews rolling down the velvety petals,
Soothe the green leaves, yearning for this nectar.
Ahh! The envious thorns have pricked my finger.
Hmm, perhaps they don't want me lingering near.

In the heavenly aura of enchanting resplendence,
My soul seems enlightened in your magnificence.
You are an epitome of the Almighty's munificence;
I feel gratified in the shower of your benevolence.

Why are you so generous O! Salmon Orange Rose?
Is in this divinity, my poetry meets to your prose?
The plethora of colors with which you're blessed;
Is another aspect of your generosity towards men.

The serenity they bestow upon the restless souls;
Not only illuminate us but all in the mundane role.
Ahh! Now I realize the reason for your generosity;
Hmm, you attract all; and they eulogize your beauty.

In the temporal world, you provide tranquil ambiance;
Your hue paints all the souls in the color of happiness.
You possess the intoxicating musk of dewy fragrance;
I feel satiated in the realm of platonic transcendence.

5
Beauty And The Knight

Resting on the Knight's broad shoulder,
Tonight her amorous desires smolder.
Enchanted with the warmth of his breath;
She craves to touch his sun-kissed lips.

In mist of love and the deluge of passion,
She fails to hide the sensual temptation.
But, when he gently kisses her forehead;
She blushes, and her shy face turns red.

Thinking what would happen with her
When he bites her soft, and supple lips;
Perhaps tonight, winged time would halt;
When they will immerse in love so deep.

He caresses her long silky strands of hairs;
As if he explores stars in the heavenly fair.
Relishing the Midas touch of her bosoms,
He knows tonight their love will blossom.

In subdued radiance of her divine beauty,
He desires to clench her chiseled body.
Looking stealthy at their locked fingers,
Tonight her misty eyes will be harbingers.

Contemplating what will happen with him
when she would leave before the morning;
Perhaps, then his heart beats would stop.
From his inconsolable eyes, tears will drop.

6
Pleasure is a Treasure Beyond Measure

Pleasure is a treasure beyond measure;
A priceless gift of Lord to all creatures.
In mechanical life, everybody is occupied;
Now a day's simpletons are not satisfied.

They all wish to accumulate money more;
As if they had not seen better days before!
Materialistic humanity's thirst is boundless;
The cravings for prosperity in life is endless.

Beneath thick layers of covetousness and desire,
Their lust for opulence is the smoldering fire.
All are in blind race to gather worldly medallions;
Despite the knowledge, they remain in oblivion.

But one day when they would get tired in this race;
They'll repent for being trapped in the elusive maze.
Possibly destiny may give them another chance;
But the time they missed may never come again.

It's not wise to do mistake and then learn from it;
Learning from other's mistake is a better thing.
Inner happiness is the pleasure we should nourish;
Then only humankind's life will happily flourish.

The pleasure drawn from worldly luxury will wane;
But those unceasing inner joy will remain same.
If we wish to lead the life of heavenly pleasure,
We should cherish this joy as a priceless treasure.

7
Towering Spirit

In the unending struggle for existence,
We all are fighting to sustain relevance.
Sometimes our jovial spirit loses its pace;
It is tough to be calm in this arduous race.

In the mortal life, all have a ray of hope
that ushers them to the tumultuous road.
Don't forget the days will be never same,
Strive to hone the skills, to stay motivated.

In the life's vast ocean of pain and agony,
Be prepared to face the tides of adversity.
Your towering spirit can triumph over
the trials and tribulations tremendously.

In long journey always keep the spirit high;
In the end, all with firm resolve will survive.
Read the story of revered heroes of the life;
Their journey was full of trouble and strife.

Still, they didn't run away from the battlefield;
History treasures eulogy of their heroic deeds.
Those who fight hardships will be remembered,
History salutes those who never bowed head.

8
Paradise of Earth

Welcome to the paradise of earth;
Where life is the synonym of mirth.
Amid profuse blooming in serene dale,
Let's become part of this hypnotic tale.

In the tiny country of mighty mountains,
Bask in the glory of sapphire fountains.
Look at the picturesque cabins in the woods,
And the pristine lake in your neighborhood.

Isn't this a garden of Eden, we always dream?
In nature's lap, life attains the joy, supreme.
I cherish each moment spent in this heaven;
I may never get a chance to eulogize it again.

Far away from the world of professionalism,
Restless heart craves for the divine mysticism.
Confused with my affinity to the serendipity,
My so-called friends may consider it stupidity.

Away from those eyes I wish to be in oblivion;
Where my soul is part of the ethereal celebration.
Some people may consider it an act of escapism;
But I wish to listen to my soul's soothing rhythm.

Let my heart decide what I expect from the life;
I am in search of peace beyond elusive vibes.
I wish to stay forever in that paradise of earth;
Where I can envision my perfect world.

9

The Dusky Beauty

Enticing the world with her curvaceous shape,
Her soft lips have the flavor of crushed grapes.
Look at her lustful eyes and desperate desires;
Perhaps, tonight on the bed, she will set the fire.

Amidst the smoky haze, she is in search of prey;
A man of the broad chest, with whom she can play.
She is aware of her wrong impression in the world;
Where her character has been painted blurred.

Ignoring the superficial morality of this society,
She enjoys the taunts on her lousy personality.
In the double-faced world of pseudo-idealism,
Dusky beauty sees the life through her prism.

10
The Earth Has Music For Those Who Listen

The earth has music for those who listen;
All we need is freedom from lust's prison.
This temptation is never-ending wilderness;
Why do we run behind pseudo happiness?

Life is a synonym for growth in simplicity;
But we link it with the greed of prosperity.
Though we pretend to praise Lord's artistry;
We seldom embrace His colorful diversity.

Love is the music in symphony of our life;
But we never sing and dance to its rhythm.
In the blind race of superficial attainment;
At last, we will receive the disappointment.

I always doubt on this so-called cognizance;
Why has it failed to soothe souls in distress?
Perhaps the fault is in our ambiguous vision;
Why is success everyone's dream mission?

To relish the resplendence in the mortal life,
we need to enjoy the music of positive vibes.
In the cacophony of lust, hatred, and desires,
Contentment can extinguish this blazing fire.

Life is not that complicated, as we perceive;
Not a scary roller-coaster ride as we imagine,
All those who are aware of the absolute truth;
Can only enjoy the divine music of the earth.

11
Nature's Panoramic Frame

Have you ever seen nature's panoramic frame?
When the roaring waterfall kisses the blue lake.
Dreaming of the magical moments of confluence;
They dance in the joy before surrendering them.

These streams of Elixir have solaced the mankind;
But now we have no time to listen to their chimes.
They are the symbol of eternal love and continuity;
Perhaps flowing down this course since the eternity.

And what to tell about the lake waiting for them?
They must be contemplating about the convergence.
Relishing the splendiferous view of this paradise,
I wish to capture each beautiful moments in sight.

Have you ever seen nature's this panoramic frame?
When in the lap of mountains, you see an azure lake.
Draped in lush green velvet of the heavenly terrain;
The rocky stalwarts are the epitome of perseverance.

In this kaleidoscope of nature, all colors mingle,
And in the placid lake, you hear the mystical jingle.
Humankind imprisoned in his monochromatic life,
Gape at the resplendence of nature with a bleak smile.

In the blind race of greed, they have lost their sheen;
And now tired of this ordeal, they are looking within.
In Almighty's created world we all had divine beauty,
we have impaired our soul, but nature retains its purity.

12
Sunday Siesta

I dream of Sunday siesta
amidst magenta flowers
in the lush green valley
Under the bliss of bowers,
Holding your soft fingers
Nestling on your shoulders
I wish to listen to the song,
the gamut of our emotions
Fluttering as sweet butterfly
will relish your love's nectar,
When you kiss my wet eyes
and touch my soft pink lips
I feel someone has rescued
me from this doomed ship
In this valley of tranquility
Beyond the elusive morality
This world may not support
But I'm happy to be an escort.

13
Blossoming Flowers

Let's envision the ecstatic earth
through the blossoming flowers.
Far away from the worldly tangle
where fatigued simpleton jingles.

Beyond those boundaries of lust,
draped in the cloak of your trust.
I wish a place in that serene vale;
A beautiful abode of my fairy tale.

Let's listen to the soft rhapsody
through the blossoming flowers.
Deep inside the celestial woods,
behind the trees, passion blooms;

Where I'll cajole your hurt heart
in green plain dotted with ferns.
I wish to slumber in the warm lap;
A velvety Dale for the midday nap.

Let's orchestrate the cool breeze
through the blossoming flowers.
Before surrendering to its charm,
dreaming of resting in your arms.

In this panoramic view of mirth
spending my life is indeed worth.
I wish to cherish the golden days
of our bonding on the scenic trail.

14
Temperance

Beneath susurration of the wet bougainvillea vines,
Let us sit and ponder about the purpose of our life.
Where blows fragrant breeze of the pure containment;
Let's savor there, the nectar of heavenly happiness.

It is the divine beauty of the truthful life of mankind;
That separates his humanity from the world of vices.
Whatever desires smolder inside our restless heart;
We should contemplate about the path that is worth.

Beneath the pink umbrella of the bougainvillea vines;
Let's resolve to imbibe the noble temperance in our life.
Truth's modesty distinguishes it from the haughty vices;
All we need to lead the worldly life on the principled line.

Abstinence is bit easy but practicing temperance is hard;
It is the arduous challenge to bring this divinity inward.
Temperance is the synonym of self-control and diligence;
It tells humankind; the real definition of the felicitous life.

There is a very thin line between truth and falsehood;
It is upon us to adjudicate what we embrace in our life.
If we wish to cross the ocean of irresistible temptations;
Temperance is the boat that can take us to the destination.

15
Share The Happiness

In this mundane life, all crave for inner happiness;
Despite this cognizance, we all nourish loneliness.
Perfect life is elusive dream, a restless soul's desire;
In harsh reality, the hope is an inextinguishable fire.

When you see recent past, days were not the same;
Vanilla wall of bygone days had the imperfect frame.
What to say about the life we are leading at present,
Despite relentless mind, face enacts to look pleasant.

Let future remain a mystic fantasy, my dear heart!
In this arduous odyssey, one has to witness dearth.
If there are several reasons to be sad and gloomy;
This life also gives a chance to be free and happy.

If sadness is vast ocean, Felicity is also not trivial;
In the law of nature, all can be happy and jovial.
See innocent faces of your family and loved ones!
Who always look at you with the high expectation.

Close your weary eyes and see who appears first,
Go and find happiness right there, O moron heart!
Your dear ones will be reason for exultant cheer;
For every complex problem, solutions linger near.

In simpleton's life, happiness is the key to success;
In this long journey, gather strength from distress.
Happiness never decreases by being shared to all;
Candle's life will not shorten if it lit lamps more.

16
Veracity

Veracity is the real essence of the morality;
It's a virtuous present draped in the divinity.
In the world of ambiguity and elusive vision;
It instills in our mind; the power of discretion.
Parent, teachers and the elders impart it to us;
Still, we seldom use in the glitter of the world.

Veracity is the heart and soul of the humanity;
It is the golden key to the world of prosperity.
From the other people, we expect truthfulness;
but in embracing honesty, we show reluctance.
Credulous and crafty traits corrode noble soul;
Despite this cognizance, we prefer negative role.

Veracity gives mankind the glimpse of serenity;
In search of this, he has traversed the eternity.
Our values may shake in the vertiginous climb;
But this robust attribute strengthens our mind.
If we wish to attain the ultimate enlightenment;
We must teach mankind about its significance.

17

Serenity Amid diversity

In the mundane world, painted in vast diversity,
Let's experience the glory of nature's serenity.
Though variation is perfect mirror of our society,
Still, the beauty of nature lies in the divine unity.
Why humankind always forget God's generosity?
This panorama is also one aspect of His creativity.
Don't expect everyone to follow a chosen way,
Everyone has a distinct way to be jovial and gay.
Key of serenity lies in attaining inner happiness,
Strength is not in the similarity but is in difference.

18

Beauty is truth and truth is beauty

From the peak of the Himalayan snow-covered mountain;
I behold the nature's panorama of divine resplendence.
I smiled and murmured the chiasmus of Poet John Keats;
"Beauty is truth and truth is beauty" fits with this scene.

The colossal wall of mighty rock and its chiseled chest;
Perhaps eulogize the beauty and the definition at its best.
Beauty lies in the eyes of beholder, is what we've learned;
My rendezvous with beauty was awaited by jaunty heart.

In this mesmerizing view, beauty mingles with life's truth;
As if on vast canvas brown and white colors are imbued.
And the color of truthful beauty evolved from confluence;
Can paint the mankind in the enchanting hue of happiness.

From the peak of the Himalayan snow-covered mountain;
I reminisce about truthful odyssey despite many ordeals.
The sheen of my eyes and glow of my skin at this height;
know how my enlightened soul and heart are entwined.

The truth's aura and magnificent halo defines its beauty;
Those who have embraced this virtue can relish it fully.
Sometimes truth sounds harsh in the glitter of the world;
But truth's beauty never fades despite rest all are blurred.

Truth enhances the radiant glow of its follower's beauty;
In the shadow of truth's beauty, let's do our earthly duty.
These two virtues resembles the bond of heart and soul;
We need to embrace their essence and perform our role.

19
The Dream I Still Cherish to Realize

Far from the interrogating eyes of my husband and the family;
Sitting near the tranquil lake, I am thinking about my destiny.
The doctor's words, in the hospital, were still hurting my mind.
The tangerine skyline seems as melancholy as my sobbing heart.

Since last ten years, I have been dreaming of becoming a mother;
But I have seen smithereens of it at the end of every month.
Taunts of society and heart ripping jibes of my so-called family,
have forced me to run away from them and hide in this solitude.

It is the dream of the motherhood which I still cherish to realize;
A divine feeling to hold in my trembling hand, a gurgling child.
But in the life, some dreams do not take the shape of the reality;
And perhaps I am the chosen one for this role, by my destiny.

Failing to gulp the rising emotions and pangs of broken heart;
I am looking for solace in the reflection of the orange-hued sun.
But look at my luck! It is also hiding behind the crimson twilight;
Perhaps there is no sunny morning after my never-ending night.

All sermons and wisdom look insignificant when the soul cries;
For others, it may be trivial, but this is the only dream of my life.
When I look at my reflection in the quivering water of this lake;
I find it darker than the shadows of the ferns and vine at the bank.

Wiping the tears, I look at wristwatch, which asks me to return;
Among the same disdainful eyes from where I wanted to escape.
But as long as I have a hope, I will dare to dream of a complete life;
Thinking about my frail spirit, I heave a sigh and smile at the sun.

20
Smiling Buddha

Venerable monks gathered near the old sacred fig tree;
Where Buddha was present far from the mundane spree.
Divine Halo of Lord had brightened the misty ambiance;
Supreme God enlightened all souls with divine radiance.

An inquisitive monk put forward an interesting question;
Other pupils too chorused with same curious expression.
What is the best way to cherish the knowledge forever?
In the journey beyond life, no one carries this treasure.

Even, a merchant doesn't give bounty as a gracious favor;
What would be our profit if we impart it to the others?
If his karmic nature is to earn benefit from all that he sold;
Wouldn't it be folly to donate freely, our priceless gold?

This wisdom must be acquired by interested humankind;
Today, we monks have this complicated question in mind.
Though we sound a bit self-centered, our respected Lord;
We know in the Karmic cycle; nothing comes free of cost.

Lord Buddha smiled softly looking at the restless souls;
His aura was solacing everyone present in worldly roles.
Bestow your invaluable wisdom to the deserving people;
Hiding this treasure is hard, imparting is pretty simple.

Transfer your divine knowledge without any expectation;
All will be grateful to you for giving the strong foundation.
Nature takes care of the complex cycle of the give and take;
All mortals should know that their karma is only at stake.

Our thoughts shape us, and we become what we think;
Spreading this awareness is better than any ethereal drink.
He forwarded his hand towards the queue of earthen lamps;
Gleaming lights were dancing amid evening dews and damps.

If you lit the lamp for others, it will also brighten your path;
If you transfer the knowledge, its strength will be enhanced.
Seed sown by you will ultimately become a fruitful tree;
You don't need to be raindrop if you have the potential of a sea.

21
Water Lilies And The Japanese Bridge

A perfect paradise of Mr. Claude Monet's dream,
Nature's vast canvas painted in the fern green;
Welcome to the fascinating world of the pink
hued water lilies and arched Japanese bridge.

The enchanting panorama of the green beauty
entices me to descend into the portrait of ebony.
Ah! I wish to reach closer to the wooden bridge;
Hmm, I will have to wade across the quiet lake.

Perhaps the intoxicating aroma of the pink lilies
will usher me to the enchanting curved bridge.
The overgrown ferns and the exotic green plants
look exuberant in their reflections on the water.

Now, I find myself standing on mildewed bridge;
Maybe no one walked across it for many weeks.
When I look around, nestling on the bridge rails;
I see you, calling me from the edge of the frame.

Why do you want me to come out of the portrait?
I yearn to stay forever amid the lush green foliage.
Sometimes I'm envious of you, my dear Mr. Monet!
Because you relished the divinity that I still crave.

22

Your Sweet Memories

Far away from the pleasant hug of love,
Under this tree, I am consoling my heart.
Why do you always come into my mind?
And my soul submerges into you forever.

O! Love don't pretend that you don't
get the restless vibes of a desperate heart.
When we used to live together in village;
You always had queries; I had complaints.

But now when you are many miles away,
My life is sweetened by sweet memories.
Your incessant chat and melodious songs,
Still, resonate in my heart and the soul;

But now when your fragrance is far away;
Your memories keep heart elated and gay.
Thanks a lot for those sweetest memories;
They usher me to the lane beyond agony.

How can I ever forget your voice and song?
The fairy musical of your pleasing cadence.
Those mellifluous memories will never fade;
Whether I am in the plain or the grey lane.

23

The Fun of Rustics is Often on The Run

The fun of rustics is often on the run;
All we need to be brave and stubborn.
When I find myself at mazy crossroad;
Poor soul contemplates about my role.

Am I destined to be a meek spectator
Or the one who wades through ocean?
Why am I afraid of the fate unknown?
Isn't it a folly to kill the dreams, before?

Unless we'll not explore the length of roads
How can we anticipate it is tiresome run?
Have you ever seen the farmer in the field?
He works relentlessly with the positive spirit.

If he'll be apprehensive about the result;
Then how can he relish the joy of his efforts?
See the long queue of the provident ants;
They enjoy the life beyond apprehensions.

Those who stride on the less trodden road;
Always emerge at the end; the satiated souls.
Don't think too much before vertiginous climb;
You will never enjoy the thrills of the height.

From seashore, you can view only its beauty;
But you will rejoice amid the dancing waves.
We can't always be in the closet of ifs and buts;
We'll have to come out and enjoy the life's fun.

Far away from the planning and calculations;
Why can't we walk on the untraversed roads?
All we need to keep aside, our burdened mind;
Then only we can relish the beauty of the life.

24
Exuberance

Exuberance of the blossoming yellow rose,
Teaches us how to live in a world of thorns.
People who are optimistic and exuberant,
Can cross the ocean of turbulent emotions.

Life has never been the bed of rose petals;
It is not Utopia, where all dream to settle.
All crave for perfect world full of happiness;
But life's canvas is dabbed with the tint of pain.

Exuberant souls are those who admire nature;
Despite mundane tangles envision their future.
Those who are in general, joyously unrestrained;
At crucial points are prudent and self-contained,

Exuberance doesn't mean that we forget our role;
Every emotion of mankind must have self-control.
Beauty of life lies in the colors of many shades;
It is a kaleidoscope that emits flickering radiance.

Whenever I look at you, blossoming yellow rose;
You add ornamental words in life's realistic prose.
Despite cognizance that tomorrow you will wilt;
You seem exuberant as if you are in eternal bliss.

25
Twitter of The Yellow Warbler

Listen to the twitter of the yellow warbler;
Resting on the branch, adorned with flowers.
When I start the day amid mundane spree;
You watch me, from the roadside oak tree.

And when I look into your inquisitive eyes;
I find many questions, but I don't have a reply.
What can I explain to the blissful yellow bird?
When there is farrago everywhere in the world.

Unlike you, our human mind is always restless;
Perhaps, we have made our daily life complex.
Real happiness lies in ignoring mundane pain;
Still, we are in a mad rush despite cognizance.

Leading a smooth and straight life is not a sin;
Only amidst ordeal, you can't get eternal bliss.
Happiness is the divine gift bestowed upon us;
We need to embrace it in life to relish the mirth.

O! blissful yellow warbler on twittering spree;
Can you provide me shelter on your oak tree?
Far from the relentless rush of this harsh world;
I also wish to fly in the blue sky as an elated bird.

26
The Land of Ecstasy

Welcome to the spectacular garden of Eden;
Where all souls relish the beauty of heaven.
In our world, we do not have time for others;
You must be thinking, Here, who will greet us?
But Dear! You are in the wonderland of ecstasy;
Here angels will usher us to the flight of fantasy.

In this paradise, I am feeling a divine euphoria;
Perhaps this is the place; we named as Utopia.
I wonder how we will adapt in this wonderland;
After all, I'm not seeing anyone depressed and sad.
Let me ask this to the enchanting purple flowers;
They must have answers of all our apprehensions.

O! dear mortal souls, this place is similar to yours;
The difference is, how you have painted the soul.
God has not divided universe as earth and heaven;
It is our karma which converted our world into hell.
Wherever you will see, souls submerged in ecstasy;
That mirthful place will be a wonderland of fantasy.

You can also relish ecstasy in the mundane world;
All you need to receive pleasure from other's mirth.
Ecstasy will be doubled if you share your happiness;
Then you will find on earth everything as in heaven.
Though you all are intellectual and enlightened souls;
You need art of living in ecstasy, not heavenly abode.

27
Magnanimity

Magnanimity is the virtue of the blessed souls;
An attribute that enlightens all in the worldly role.
In this nature, everyone gets chance to offer it;
Be it plants, animals, birds or this Gulmohur tree.
Though plants struggle hard to grow their fruit;
Never shy away from giving it to those in need.

See the herd of cows engrossed in the eternal bliss;
But when the little child cries they offer their milk.
Have you ever heard music in the chirping of birds?
These twittering birds usher path to all who are lost.
And how can I describe this dancing Gulmohar tree?
I see in it the perfect image of divine magnanimity.

Am I lucky to get the glimpse of our nature's opulence?
Or it is just a flight of fantasy in this illusive ambiance.
Oh, My heart! I know you always dominate my mind;
Today I wish to listen to you through the wind chime.
See, my prudent mind promptly whispered in my ears;

This is not a dream; You live in a magnanimous nature.
In the mundane tangles; mankind acts as self-centered;
And they hardly notice the divinity of splendid nature.
If you wish to enjoy this virtue of divine magnanimity;
You should never hesitate to help like Gulmohur tree.

28
Unplugged Mirth

I am the blue bird of the crimson world;
A haunting canvas painted in the blood.
Believe me; I am not a sadist as you think;
But, this world is dotted with the red ink.
The cities and villages which I traverse;
I get the glimpse of a melancholy human.
Though I don't have complicated tangles;
Am I novice to understand human's angle?
Now you can only explain how to get mirth;
Dear tree! When all are in pain in the world.

O! My dear blue-hued bird with colorful wing;
Human life is not that complicated as you think.
Unlike us, they have the unquenchable thirst;
They never hesitate to spoil elated and gay souls.
Though God has bestowed upon all His opulence;
Mankind is in the mad rush to grab other's share.
If you wish to see them submerged in the mirth;
You must spread this awareness to all on the earth.
Unplugged mirth is the attribute that all possess.
But unlike us, they are calculative in expressing it.

29
Awakening

Why did you wake me from my old dreams?
I don't wish to live in this world without him;
When I'll get his glimpse from the hills yonder?
Then again I'll have to sob in the dark corner.

What sort of awakening are you trying to teach?
When you see this widowed, in the intense grief.
Still, you preach me, Oh sympathetic China Rose!
Can't you see my raining eyes and burning soul?

The soul's awakening which you teach me today;
Can't bring back my those mirthful golden days.
If the awakening means to return to pain again;
Nah I don't wish to attain that unreal cognizance.

All the prudence and pragmatism erased from this mind;
The day, he left for heavenly abode, leaving me behind.
Please let me moan in the darkest place of this earth;
Only amidst the warmth of old memories, I get the mirth.

O, dear lady! I know the condition of your sobbing heart!
Still, you need healing of awakening to live in the world.
Though truth is bitter medicine for all the grieving souls;
All who embrace this truth, they are the awakened souls.

You will have to come to the sunshine from the night of grief;
Willing or unwillingly you have to lead your life without him.
All I wish to awaken the soul lost in the chasm of deep pain;
So that your dear family and friends can see your smile again.

30
Serenity Within Us

Far away from the sight of disgusting world;
In the magnificent land of unrestrained mirth.
Will you be with me in that beautiful serenity?
Where I will be in your warmth till the eternity.

When I watch the rapacious souls on the prowl;
I huddle behind the tropical tree and large ferns.
In the world where struggle for existence is destiny;
I wish to reside in the blissful land of the serenity.

In my eyes, you may find thousands of complaints;
But how can I be, in this cacophony until the end?
Listen to my desperation, urging for your company;
To the exotic wonderland of the heavenly serenity.

Although I love you very much, O my sweetheart!
It is my duty to show the mirror of the real world.
When your soul is calm despite being in tempest;
And you aren't envious of the other's big success.

Believe me; the confused soul caged in your body;
Will relish the perpetual mirth amid the serenity.
Blissful happiness resides within everyone's heart;
We need to awaken the poor soul, in the hibernation.

When we enjoy the rhythm of our love's symphony;
That moment you will attain ecstasy in the serenity.
In the surreal serenity, let's be together till the death;
We can relish the eternal bliss in this real world itself.

31
Lost Love

When I saw him sleeping with someone else;
I resolved that we would never meet again.
Oh, my poor heart why did you bring me here?
Amidst this tranquility, these eyes shed tears.

Though I know, one should not visit old lanes;
In this serenity, I feel his warm breath again.
In the breeze of my lost love's intense lyrical;
My inconsolable soul is yearning for a miracle.

Though I am not ashamed of this desperation;
But how to free my soul from his captivation?
Once you fall in charm of your adorable mate;
Despite harsh realities, the stupid heart waits.

At this bench where I used to nestle in his arms;
I can imagine; he is enjoying someone's charm.
O wind! Why don't you inform him about my life;
Doesn't he ever remember my love and its vibes?

See! I have worn same red dress; he gifted to me;
O autumn breeze! Tell him I am waiting for him.
Look at the miserable condition of desperate soul;
Please inform him to release me from his control.

I know the world considers this as my stupid act;
but those moments of love I can never forget.
Though he must be enjoying in his new abode;
Still, I wish to cherish my priceless lost love.

32
The Picture of Past

Long back ago, far away, in the dense woods,
There was a church in our neighborhood.
I used to visit that place to worship my Lord;
Along with elder sister; the best in the world.

We listened to the symphony of wild nature;
On the serene lake, we scribbled our signature.
How much I miss those moments of our life;
Today I am at the same place with wet eyes.

Perhaps destiny had some other plans for me,
And I had to go far away from those tall trees;
After many summers and the winters passed;
I dared to visit the old church that still haunts.

The edifice of the white church is still intact;
But it has lost forever; Its former magnificence.
When I see the placid lake, I get her glimpse;
And at the broken trunk where we used to sit.

Behind the Crimson gate, she was dishonored;
And after the brutal sin, they dumped her here.
When the rapacious red demons left the place;
I saw her as lifeless body floating on the lake.

The intermittent flashes of past hurt my heart;
but what to do if I've been an inseparable part.
I wish to enter this framed picture of my past;
and paint it afresh with the hue of happiness.

Though my imaginations dominate my mind;
I can still hear her sweet whispers from behind.
Looking at the same old church of the wilderness;
I can envision, my sister, singing in eternal bliss.

33
Prose on Our Love

Could you please write a prose on our love?
As they say, you have mastered in the word.
I have the desire to see you writing a tome;
As a skilled artist chisels the unshaped stone.

Though you've plenty of time to write on others;
But when I ask, you always have excuses bigger.
As there is always thick darkness below the lamp;
It seems I would be waiting for a prose till the end.

At the time of our marriage you made big promises;
See! After many years, you've forgotten all of them.
I want you to pick best adjectives, verbs, and adverbs;
And write a soulful epic on me, O! sculptor of words.

Your earnest desire always brings smile on my face;
Believe me! From your eyes, I've stolen many verses.
When you linger around me, I get fresh breeze of love;
That inspires me to write the soulful poetry and prose.

If you read the similes and metaphors carefully in them;
You will find the description of your persona in them.
And have you read my historical fiction that I wrote lately?
You will see your glimpse in many clauses and phrases.

I am just an artist of the words; not a persuasive orator;
You must have got the answer if you are a good reader.
When the two souls are entwined in the bond of love;
Then emotion travels from eye to eye; without the words.

34
Inspiration

In the heavenly garden of
orange-hued African daisy;
I am looking into your eyes
And you're driving me crazy.

Although, the world always
considers it as my stupidity;
But I must confess I'm always
inspired by your divine beauty.

I hope my heart beats transmit
to you, through my Rhapsody;
Still, why don't you look happy
in this garden of heavenly glory.

I was contemplating about you
and your source of motivation.
It is insult to noble cognizance,
If my beauty is your inspiration.

My glowing skin and supple lips,
Will lose sheen and get wrinkled;
Do you still think my old body
will be the source of inspiration?

If you have to draw inspiration
then look upon deeds of all souls.
Those great souls inspire the world;
who have spent years in hard work.

Beauty is just an enticing illusion;
They aren't the source of motivation.
The desire to grow with dedication;
My pal should be your inspiration.

35
Contentment

Contentment is origin of eternal bliss;
A virtue that paves the path to peace.
Contended humankind enjoys the life;
Even if he is amid the tempest of strife.

In noble pursuit of divine contentment;
Revered souls attained enlightenment.
Ram, Krishna, Buddha and Jesus Christ;
We will find their virtues in all the Epics.

Contentment doesn't stop us to desire;
It advises us controlling its intense fire.
For growth, we've to be object-oriented;
It teaches us always be calm until the end.

With balanced life and contented soul;
Noble people perform the worldly role.
Though we find pleasure in happiness;
Even in agony, we can see contentment.

In the turbulent journey of human life;
This virtue facilitates them to survive.
Everyone in the world should understand;
Success and failure are the universal facts.

Contentment is the real wealth of nature;
Those who opt it will have a bright future.
If we are complacent with what we possess;
Then all souls can be enlightened, Perhaps.

36
Equanimity

Despite facing hundreds of frightful tempests;
We should never lose composure and equanimity.
From glorious Mythology to recent world History,
Only balanced souls have attained this divinity.

It has always enlightened the desperate humankind;
and instills in them, the sacred nectar of humanity.
When mortal people lose mind on small or big issues;
This divine virtue balances the upsurge of emotions.

Every religion of the world teaches this Philosophy;
Humankind should always embrace the equanimity.
This attribute generates feeling of the detachment;
And only those souls can relish eternal happiness.

As after the tempest, we always see settling of dust;
Despite all the turmoil and outbursts, our life adjusts.
From the aureole of Lord, many attributes radiates;
They all bless mortal lives with their magnificence.

Equanimity free us from the net of worldly reactions;
A never-ending tug of war between conflicting notions.
Though this virtue ushers us to the realm of salvation;
We seldom embrace it with sincerity and full dedication.

37
Cherish Your Dreams

Cherish your dreams till your last breath;
Life gives us a chance to fulfill our dreams.
Dreams are compilation of hidden desires;
which float in the mind when we shut eyes.

Though we can speculate on origin of dream;
But we know that it boosts our self-esteem.
From childhood to the golden age of the life;
Our dreams accompany and soothe the mind.

In complex labyrinth of the temporal world;
We hardly get any time to listen to our heart.
When we feel disheartened and distressed;
Our dreams sprout the radiance of happiness.

In the dark realm of heart-wrenching realism;
Dreams usher us to the path of luminance.
Those who consider them just a wistful fancy;
Perhaps do not know, dreams become a reality.

All we need to embrace a pragmatic approach;
Then only we can move on the path of growth.
Though dream vanishes when we open our eyes;
Somewhere in our conscience they flutter and fly.

Almighty has given divine power to human beings;
To carve their splendid future on what they dream.
Cherish your dream till you end the life's journey;
They will always motivate you in the long odyssey.

Wizard of Poetry And Prose

He would come and paint her restless heart
In the lustful color of the amorous words.
Tonight, on velvety bed of the crimson rose,
She is waiting for Wizard of poetry and prose.
Envisioning of his warmth and sensual sighs;
Her canvas is desperate to get tinted tonight.
Eavesdropping his steps stamping the alley;
She dreams to spend a night in love's valley.

Shh! He has caught the silly beauty's blue eyes;
Perhaps he will passionately punish her tonight.
Dreaming about commingling of their verses,
Clenching the sheet of love, she looks nervous.
But he will soothe the simmering desire of her;
When he will write his quotes on her soft lips.
She'll shudder and wriggle feeling bit ashamed;
But tonight he would paint her erotic portrait.

Each passing moments are arousing her desires;
Before the climax, they will set the bed on fire.
Sometimes her heart wonders about these all;
But what to do when this feeling created by God?
It is easy to tag people based on their character;
but in love just confluence of two hearts matter.
When the world is looking for meaningful words;
She is lost in his love's precise, prose, and verse.

39
Imaginations Paint me Young

Though I'm not ashamed of my old age;
but my imaginations paint me young.
Strolling in the splendid garden of mirth;
I feel elated amidst the beauty of the earth.

When I was very young, my parents said;
Our body grows old; soul remains the same.
Under the guidance of my revered teachers,
I learned the art of living amid all the tensions.

Often disheartened by the successive failures,
I used to consider, Is my life a failed venture?
But the desires and imaginations of my heart,
Solaced my distressed soul, not to feel hurt.

They instill the hope to achieve the dreams;
Though they don't know how to implement it.
Our imaginations boost the power of the mind;
It assists us to leave harsh tangles far behind.

Imagination enhances the power of discretion;
A perfect gift by our Lord to every generation.
The chirping of birds and these colorful ferns,
In this garden's mesmeric charm, I feel young.

I often feel bewildered, seeing the cycle of life;
But my jovial soul discloses the truth behind it.
One day my tired body will go to sleep forever;
But my juvenile soul will always be felt here.

40
The Saga of Love

The saga of love is eternally elegant;
An epical journey that is magnificent.
Though many centuries have passed;
But its timeless fragrance can be felt.

Love is passion and love is the desire;
It's the warmth of the simmering fire.
Love has traversed the infinite trails;
Still, it rejuvenates all the depressed.

It creates inextinguishable conflagration;
and replenishes the ebbing emotions.
Love is the religion and love is divine;
It is a string with that we're entwined.

The saga of love is eternally elegant;
A story, written in the ink of the pain.
Though many consider it as stupidity;
Those in love can infer its real feeling.
Love is the ocean and love is the waves;
It is unfathomable and difficult to wade.
Love has been witness of World History;
The reason for wars, deceit and misery.

It arouses the desire of accomplishment;
The dream of confluence and attainment.
Love is Lord and love is the eternal bliss;
It is the pivot on which humanity rests.

41
Grandeur of Love

The serpentine trail of mountainous beauty;
Baffles me; entices me and perhaps binds me.
And what to say about the crimson-hued ferns;
They look captivating amid the gyrating petals.

This place seems far from my hut in the Prairies;
Have I stepped into the world of lovely fairies?
Nah! How can fairies descend on the awful earth?
Perhaps Lord has bestowed on me Grandeur of love.

Yeah, this is the panorama of the splendid beauty;
Painted with the hue of love, passion and divinity?
When I relish the resplendence of this land;
I wonder why we all run behind human whims?

The love, we search in the mortals, is infatuation;
Eternal love can be seen somewhere in our nature.
The feeling that instills in us a divine satisfaction;
That is the real love and its precise definition.

Grandeur of love can be eulogized by those in love;
To envision its beauty, first, understand this word.
Love is an unfathomable feeling of the mankind;
Only after relishing its beauty, it can be defined.

42

Embrace Both Pain And Pleasure For Growth

One quote always resonates in my thoughts;
Embrace both pain and pleasure for growth.
It had been shared with me by an old friend;
Who always observed me in the deep distress.

I gazed at his face; Bit confused and surprised;
I knew that he had hinted the key of stable life.
Never be too much elated that's hard to handle;
Or submerge into grief when fortune dwindles.

Our life should be as simple as a straight line;
Grief and joy shouldn't change the course of life.
If you are in deep pain; look for the silver lining;
If you are delighted; remember! It has an ending.

Mirth attended after agony is always sweetest;
Arduous ordeal always prepares us for the best.
Embrace both pain and pleasure for the growth;
Then you can envision life beyond monochrome.

43
Glorious Achievement

When I search your face in the firmament;
I feel you are my life's glorious achievement.
You would be chirping behind the Azure cloud;
Perhaps stealthily watching me from behind.
The day you departed to the heavenly abode;
I have been searching your image since then.
All persuade me to forget you as an old pain;
Why I cherish you as a glorious achievement?
When all flaunt the vast opulence they possess;
You may see your father submerged in distress.

My dear daddy, you are simply the best in world;
When I see you in grief, I do not have the word.
As you always consider me as your achievement;
I too remember you as the source of my merriment.
Though my journey was bit short, I am happy;
In your blessing and love, I get divine serenity.
Whatever worldly luxury all other may possess;
Our eternal bonding always has been priceless.
I am fortunate to get an adorable father like you;
I will always be the glorious achievement of you.

44
Adolescence

In the enchanting days of the adolescence;
Soaring desires conflict with our prudence.
Though at this age we have little awareness;
But these are the days filled with liveliness.

After getting full attention in our childhood;
We step into a dreamy world of adolescence.
It's a fantasy world with the hue of some truth;
Where we learn the challenges of adulthood.

In this period of rapid cognitive development;
Whatever we learn, is our lifetime investment.
This transition teaches many lessons of the life;
It shapes our mind to survive amidst the strife.

Though these golden days have vast potential;
We may find; worldly glitter more influential.
Enthralled with the arrival of physical puberty;
Some of us can indulge in the act of immaturity.

Though we may attain momentary happiness;
Mistakes of the tender age put us in the stress.
Learn from burgeoning beauty of Bougainvillea;
Life has never been a long sojourn in Arcadia.

One day when we will enter the young age;
Lessons of adolescence will give us guidance.
Let's celebrate the grandeur of this gleeful days;
And relish its youthfulness and resplendence.

45
Tinsel Town's Neighborhood

In the scintillating Tinsel town's neighborhood
Where hungry souls are in search of little food;
Do I belong to the society of emotional numbness?
Where everyone seems submerged in indifference.

Despite being just spectator of thousands of skeletons,
How does humankind talk to go beyond the horizon?
Amidst boastful advertisements of the shining India,
The harsh realism often fades in the glitz of media.

Today I saw him eating the leftover on banana leaf;
Perhaps this garbage was his first and the last meal.
Where all run behind the glitter of glamour valley;
He is often seen strolling near the rusted trash trolley.

This heart-wrenching reality is the irony of our world;
Where deaths from hunger is still a serious concern.
The glitter of Tinsel town pricks at my gloomy eyes;
Somewhere in its vicinity, lives struggle to survive.

46
Stigma

Afraid of the horrendous society and its fierce anger;
He hides the face in the dark, claustrophobic chamber.
Not sure, how to save the dwindling life and self-respect;
He has pledged to survive despite social stigma of AIDS.

47

We Are Born of Love, Love is Our Mother

We are born of love; love is our mother,
Despite this cognizance, we always bother.
Though we start the journey with morals high,
Somewhere in midway, we go astray in the life.

Love is the lantern that ushers us on this trail,
Instilling positivity in a soul, depressed and frail.
I know you may consider it just another sermon;
But I have witnessed the aspect of life in person.

In this mad rush of success, I saw enemies in all;
Always paranoid about my imaginary downfall.
One day I resolved to change my way of thinking;
And tried to love all; learned the art of forgiving.

Though it was hard to remain in idealistic cloak;
But this philosophical doctrine, I planned to opt.
It taught me; we should not lose trust and hope;
Many colors prevail in the life's kaleidoscope.

Today when all are striving for temporal mirth;
You see everywhere benevolent love's dearth.
Almighty has bestowed upon us all His opulence;
He expects us to spread love's magical radiance.

Love begets love; It should be motto of our life
Why waste this priceless time on trivial fights?
We have come to the mortal world to spread love;
It should be the goal of everyone in the universe.

48
I Breathe to Live With You

After hectic hours at work
Far from disdainful smirk
When I return sweet home
To lead life in monochrome

Where mind yearns to shed
Onerous burdens from head
Resting on the ebony chair
I hear murmurs in my ear

And a slight nudge on knee
Pull me out of worldly spree
On opening my weary eyes
I see sole purpose of my life

A source of ethereal energy
My baby is standing near me
Sunshine of my small world
I see God in you, little girl!

You create an isle of smile
In vast sea of sustenance
My little princess Shamita!
I breathe to live with you.

49
Beauty

When you say that my beauty is bliss;
And on my supple lips, you give a kiss.
I contemplate about this amorous love;
Is this just a momentary infatuation?

Could you please tell me, my soul mate?
Is this enchanting beauty, a mistake?
Though you have persuaded my heart;
Still, I yearn to hear the truth from you.

These doubts often resonate in my mind;
But what to do when my love is so blind?
O! dream merchant of lush green vale;
Tell me! Is our unnamed love a fairy tale?

Perhaps you haven't understood my love;
And my eyes did not convince your heart.
Your beautiful and pure soul is what I love;
Searching beauty in mortal body mere lust.

These blooming flowers and green ferns;
Their beauty is in the divinity and mirth.
Beauty always lies in the eyes of beholder;
I am in love with the beauty of your soul.

When I shower affection through the kiss;
Believe! In your warmth; I get pure bliss.
O! my sweet damsel of this splendid dale;
My love story is more than a dreamy tale.

50
Enraptured Existence

There are plethora of diverse colors,
As far as my astonished eyes can see.
And amongst these variegated tulips,
I envision enraptured existence of me.

In the panorama of multi-hued valley,
My heart savors nuggets of wisdom.
This inspiring Vista gives the glimpse
of Almighty's divine celestial kingdom.

The twirling of spring blooming bulbs
remind me how magnificent our life is.
Perhaps amidst these dancing flowers,
I can weave exquisite tapestry as a wiz.

Am I the chosen one by revered Angels
Who usher me to the path of liveliness?
Or perhaps a rhapsody hymn by me
for vivid nature's enraptured existence.

Whatever is the reason of my presence;
I'm desperate to relish its resplendence.
As body needs breathing for the survival
Pure spirit is needed for spiritual revival.

Breeze whispers to me with a loving kiss;
I am fortunate to revel the heavenly bliss.
Though I'll not return in this gleeful dale;
It will resonate in my mind as a fairy tale.

51
Rendezvous With Lord Ram

Beyond throttling shackles of the worldly temptation,
This brief journey ends at His heavenly destination.
Look at the carefree body, away from complex tangles,
Still, you crave for elusive life, already in shambles.

In days, months and years, loved one will move ahead,
Why do you feel your memory will remain in their head?
Your days of happiness with beloved family, now a past;
In this entire universe, life halts only soul's journey last.

Body is a glittering attire, destined for continual change;
Think about your next life, eagerly waiting to embrace.
This is ocean of temptation; you have to pass through,
Don't sob departing soul; Lord Ram awaits you.

Just think about your rendezvous with Lord Ram;
Don't burst into tears and keep your heart calm.
Experience his warm hug of boundless compassion;
Nimbus blue Lord is the name of greatest satisfaction.

Feel His effulgent halo in the sparkling misty light;
The reservoir of bliss and His glory, now in your sight.
In karmic cycle, His abode is every soul's only dream;
Who knows this may be your last chance to meet him.

Witness this golden moment of transcendental pleasure,
Don't miss the chance to cherish, this heavenly treasure.
In this eternal journey, life is a mirage and death a truth,
Don't sob departing soul; Lord Ram awaits you.

52
Blissful Poetry

Lying in the velvety lap of resplendent nature,
I am contemplating to compose a soulful verse.
From where can I get the best ornamental words?
Perhaps, I can't see them scattered in this world.

Let me write the stanza with a lovely beginning;
O! nimbus hued sky I'll borrow your silver lining.
What about the rhythm and underneath story?
I should refer my own tumultuous life's odyssey.

The poem of life is unfinished without a message;
O! azure river, can you add a thoughtful passage?
The long pine trees and the rejoicing green ferns;
I know, from you, many lessons I have to learn.

How fortunate am I, seeing myself in this heaven;
It is where life's poetry can get its resplendence.
My poem will have aroma of the fragrant breezes
and the rustling of the dancing deciduous leaves.

Some poems portray the bitter realism of the life;
Some give the glimpse of an imaginative mind.
My poetry is the tribute to the blossoming beauty
Of nature, often marred by humankind's apathy.

Despite ordeals, life gives the ability to pen down;
The fancies I nurture, through the poems of love.
Poetry is for bliss in the bloom of nature's bounty;
I feel blessed to eulogize this enchanting beauty.

The emotions oozing from the words of this verse;
May enlighten the weary souls and gloomy hearts.
The aroma of mirth spreading through the words;
May one day immortalize me and my poetic verse.

53
Sadness

How'll I live without my sweetheart?
Only he can heal my wounded heart.
O autumn breeze, please convey him;
Without his warmth, this life looks dim.

Although he has left me in the distress,
I'll not mind tag of the unwed mistress.
Amidst society's taunt and shallowness,
Now I find solace in the hidden sadness.

When my tresses caress desperate lips,
They remind me of his passionate kiss.
My closed eyes will cherish his dreams;
And my heart will always beat with him.

Remembering Midas touch of his body,
My heart will croon amorous rhapsody.
When all are running behind happiness;
I feel tranquilized in poignant sadness.

54
Blooming Passion

When he flaunts this carefree attitude;
She sobs somewhere in darkest solitude.
I feel pity for her and this one-sided love;
Is longing for someone's attention, curse?

Everyone tells if you have intense passion;
In monochrome life, some magic happens.
Please tell me the sagacious red hued rose!
What will be the fate of blooming passion?

My dear friend! though you have prudence,
But you don't apply as in this simple case.
Only that real love attains the culmination
Where both the souls have a similar passion.

Though infatuation infuses the deep passion;
But it rarely transforms into a love forever.
Flowering passion is indeed a great virtue;
But delusive expectation brings pain undue.

55
Nurturing Nature

Nurturing nature is our solemn duty;
After all, we relish its glorious beauty.
In adorned nature's vivid cornucopia,
we can envision the enthralling utopia.

Nursing the flora and fauna with love;
Gives us nature's vast bounty in return.
Though soul guide us to respect this gift;
The egotistical humankind always drifts.

We don't hesitate to exploit its opulence;
Not thinking about its dwindling radiance.
But judicious nature has profound wisdom;
Those who disrespect it lose in the system.

Sometimes I feel sorrowful and disheartened;
Despite the wisdom why we haven't changed.
Perhaps in the mad rush of materialistic glitz,
Our mind has divagated for the temporal bliss.

Nurture generous nature for symbiotic growth;
Only then we can rejoice the life at the most.
Those who care nature with immense passion;
Always receive the shower of its benevolence.

56
Love is The Elixir of Our Life

Love is the elixir of our life;
In journey marred by strife.
As food nourishes our body;
It cares souls of everybody.

Love rejuvenates our dreams;
In the harsh life full of extremes.
As dreams bring sweet smile;
It instills mirth in the dull life.

Love ushers to the zestful trail;
When we're dispirited and frail.
As Sun illuminates dark world;
It replenishes intense emotions.

Love can spellbind every heart;
Despite everyone in a mad rush.
As moonlight soothes dry eyes;
It enkindles the desires and flies.

Love doesn't happen with logic;
Though we are very calculative.
As the gleeful white water lilies;
It binds everyone with its beauty.

Love is the nectar for all mortals;
Bodies die; its charm fades never.
As warmth of breeze comforts us;
It satisfies our desperate emotions.

57

The Reign of Our Eternal Love

In the glorious reign of our eternal love;
You're fairy queen of my grateful heart.
Although we have left the mortal world;
Even now all reminisce story of our love.

As I promised to you; we will meet again;
In a paradise where the passion will rain.
Yes, In the same abode of our eternal love;
Where we will be relishing blissful mirth.

Far away from the agony, sorrow and pain;
We'll rule this heaven till the world ends.
Though our stint on the earth was short;
But, was enough to strengthen our bond.

When all were mourning on our demise;
We were elated for our confluence divine.
Now after long ordeal of distress and grief;
Our souls are basking in the glory of bliss.

In the reign of love, I'm king of your heart;
But I'll not govern; Only I'll shower my love.
In the kingdom of divine passion of romance;
I'll halt and let desperate emotions advance.

58

The Splendor of Solitude

My fatigued mind desperately yearns a recluse;
Amidst Alpine habitat and the splendid solitude.
Beneath the dancing clouds in the azure blue sky;
Gloomy realism often halts, and imaginations fly.

Although I have seen the glitter of illusive world;
Why do I get supreme solace in the solitary mirth?
In the resplendent Dale covered with green velvet;
These weary eyes relax, and exhausted body rests.

Yes, I have been dreaming of a cabin in the woods;
In the enchanting ambiance of the neighborhood.
Far away from deafening cacophony of this world;
See! The radiance of my face has finally returned.

Is this a surprise present of nature on my arrival?
Maybe rekindling of desires for my spiritual revival.
Whatsoever this tranquil solitude is bliss of my life;
I can't withstand insurmountable distress and strife.

As, for thirsty traveler, water is equivalent to nectar;
This solitude is a boon for all world-weary passengers.
When invigorating mountain air descends to the Dale;
They comfort my heart and share with me their tale.

Like me, they have escaped from the confused world;
And now blowing high-spirited in this part of the earth.
Far behind, we have left the unceasing worldly noise;
Now we are dreaming of staying forever in this mirth.

59
Path to Peace

Seeing my anxiety and restlessness;
Blooming roses whisper to my ears.
Bit surprised, I looked back at them;
Trying to decipher what they'd said.

The fragrance of roses spellbound me;
I got repose far from mundane spree.
The plethora of colors in front of me;
Bewitched my souls with its beauty.

I contemplated to ask the crimson rose;
Tell me about the path they've followed.
Their grace, charm and virtuous divinity;
Perhaps is uncommon in today's reality.

Prudent roses anticipated my confusion;
They had the answer to every question.
Only peaceful mind can usher us to goal;
In purposeful life, confusion has no role.

Peace is attained through the self-control;
It can be felt from the core, not imposed.
For an exemplary life embrace the modesty;
Never be impulsive despite the adversity.

We should learn, how to reach the goal;
Despite many thorns, roses still blossom.
Path of peace is for all enlightened souls.
They find the ray of hope even in the gloom.

60
Keep Your Mind at Peace

Always keep your mind at peace;
Your life's hope will never cease.
In tumultuous voyage of the life,
Key to success is our stable mind.

Though everyone has his own fate;
Still, we need a mind without stress.
In day to day life, we'll have to face;
An acerbic tone and its bitter taste.

Those whom we consider close mate;
They may backstab you at the end.
Life has never been a flowery prose;
Amid the pain, we've to seek repose.

Although we can't control the destiny;
But we can infuse in mind, serenity.
With composure and gracious dignity,
we can relish our life and its divinity.

Despite inheriting worldly opulence,
We can't purchase peace at any cost.
Only with complacent mind and heart;
We will be able to attain eternal mirth.

Those who maintain a peaceful mind;
They can cross every hurdle in the life.
With calm mind and clarity of vision;
We can achieve all that we envisioned.

61

The Fragrance of Magenta Lilac

The fragrance of magenta lilacs descends into my soul;
See! my envious shadow has now ditched me as before.
My spellbound senses step close to the pistils of flower;
Where they are greeted by the strong fragrance of love.

Amid the velvety petals of the gorgeous lilac bunches;
I can see your image around me that come and hug me.
In the daily life, where we don't see this divine beauty;
Perhaps love and emotion are synonyms of the divinity.

And I yearn to drape my poor soul in this eternal love;
Who knows this bond may solace my wounded heart;
My heart and soul are drenched in the lilac fragrance;
My whims and fancies are insignificant in this fragrance.

In this journey of our life, some fragrances are short-lived;
But some fragrances are forever beyond the temporal world.
The ethereal aroma of love floats in the mystical ambiance;
And my juvenile heart is fascinated with its resplendence.

Why have you controlled my all senses without my consent?
Now when I am elated, you are pushing in the same old lane.
After relishing the divine nectar of your mesmeric fragrance;
O! Dear lilac, I don't wish to endure the worldly pangs again.

62
Music is The Food of Love

Amidst the symphony of the rustling leaves;
Have you ever listened to the melody of love?
I know these blooming buds, they'll question me;
How can I ponder on it despite in worldly spree?

But it is true that I am in search of a real love;
Where can I get solace other than in these buds?
When the gush of your fragrance passes by me;
You know how desperately I need your company.

In this life, those who pretend to have moral clarity;
They will never be relevant in the realm of reality.
Though I know, the world will laugh at my stupidity;
But I relish the mirthful life amidst your divinity.

O, my restless friend! Listen to my golden words;
In chaotic mundane life, music is the food of love.
See how am I blossoming in this beautiful garden;
Along with the physical stuff, I get mental balance.

The whispering of the leaves and giggling of birds;
Never let me feel alone; I find in them, eternal love.
Like the sunshine, water and air help in my growth;
Music of ecstasy also nourishes my sensitive soul.

This music enhances my glow and mesmeric beauty;
Amid these musical notes, I compose life's symphony.
Like the flowers, the human being should also relish it;
In the music of love, you can live with apparent ease.

63
Solitary Bird

Solitary bird sitting on the pink lotus,
Wonders about the humankind's focus.
She wishes to fly and feed the nestling,
Amidst dancing fuchsia petals rustling.

She is excited but always uses her mind,
Who knows that predator may be behind!
She thinks in this struggle for existence;
The mind must have to be alert and fittest.

Solitary bird sitting on the pink lotus,
Wonders about the humankind's focus.
Why worldly people busy in this rush?
They can enjoy wetlands joyful gush.

Unlike birds, humans have all privileges,
They wish to destroy other's existence.
Even though all creatures hardly believe,
They give the slogan to live and let live.

64
Liveliness of Lovely Life

Lying on the bed of this haunting hospital,
I reminisce about bygone days of our love.
Those golden days when we dreamt a lot;
For every little success, we thanked God.

Those moments of liveliness of lovely life,
still, resonate as jovial chime in my mind.
Late night I used to return; As tired body;
Giggles of family instilled positive energy.

In the simple breakfast, lunch, and dinner,
My soul relished the paramount pleasure.
What to say about the old ancestral home,
Still, on those walls, there's the tint of love.

When you departed to the celestial abode;
Leaving me alone, in this indifferent world.
Lying on the bed of this haunting hospital,
I contemplate how to replenish old glitter.

At this old age when my sun is about to set;
I descend in old memory before last breath.
Heartfelt gratitude to Master of Universe;
You gave a chance to rejoice in the world.

I respect each moment of my golden past;
They would be my sole companion at last.
Everyone can feel liveliness of lovely life;
All we need to understand the motto of life.

65
Exhilaration

When the dark clouds shed the drops of tears;
And the peacock will dance in the green fields.
When the earth emancipates the blissful mirth;
And wet monsoon breeze will pass by my heart.

When the lightning sparkles the moonless sky;
And the sudden thunder will roar from behind.
When you come slowly to nestle in my arms;
And my restless soul will soothe in its warmth.

I wish to be part of that moment's celebration;
Where my heart will submerge in exhilaration.

When your eyes unravel your untold mystery;
And I will see your enchanting beauty finally.
When I feel the warmth of simmering passion;
And my desire will turn into the conflagration.

When your long tresses will cover my face;
And your supple pink lips will look desperate.
When you caress my gloomy and sad face;
Then I will kiss your dewy pink lips slowly.

I crave my love to climax at that destination;
Where my heart will submerge in exhilaration.

66
Sympathy

Show sympathy to the souls in agony;
Maybe they get life with your healing.
Without cleansing the mind's bitterness,
We all strive to attain inner happiness.
Try to nurture the feeling of empathy,
Lend your hand to the souls in tragedy.

Kindness is the fragrance of spirituality;
A door to the ethereal world of eternity.
It is Almighty's gift to the humankind;
But for spending it, we have no time.
If we don't shower this divine blessing,
How would others respect our feeling?

Sympathy is sweet scent of spirituality;
Its fragrance enlightens the humanity.
Care is the stepping stone to salvation;
Benevolent love ushers to redemption.
Relish the joy of wiping tearful eyes;
This heavenly happiness has no price.

67
Role of Perseverance in My Life

He left me alone when I had no support;
Probably, he did not want me in his world.
Though my eyes had thousands of questions;
But from my husband, I had no expectation.

No one came to rescue of this stranded lady;
I had to traverse many storms in this journey;
Holding my little son, I was on the crossroad.
Wondering how I would struggle in this world?

I don't know from where I got divine positivity;
I wiped my tears and fought with sealed destiny.
As a farm laborer, I worked hard to hone my skill;
I kept fighting with all the adversities till the end.

With ordinary talent and extreme perseverance;
After years of hard work, I got worldly happiness.
I'm witness of how a destitute lady can transform;
All we need the diligence to reach the destination.

After years my so-called husband came to me;
But I am not big-hearted to forgive his past deed.
Looking at the horizon and vast tangerine sky;
I thank my conscience which always guided me.

After years of struggle and pain, I got the success;
One can achieve his goals if he has perseverance.
After many failures, success is counted sweetest;
Whatever I got in the life, all due to perseverance.

68
My Senorita

When you walk in beauty on the golden sand;
I dream to unlock your close clenched hands.
Under tangerine sky, dabbed with grey paint,
My stupid heart yearns to hug your silhouette.

In the heavenly island, where we hang around;
I must admit that this ecstasy has no bounds.
Far away from the cacophony of chaotic world,
Let's dance to the tunes of the swash of waves.

My heart wishes to stay forever on La Isla Bonita;
And I crave to be your true soul mate, my senorita.

Let me bask in the glory of this golden paradise;
In the day I'll love you and cuddle you all night.
When you unfurl your grey scarf in the sea breeze;
My heart may leave me behind to get your glimpse.

Why has the Almighty created this feeling of love?
Is it a strong magnet that binds all restless couple?
Indeed, this beaming bliss of love beholds no bounds;
Maybe Supreme Lord want us to explore it and enjoy.

I envision of small abode of our love on La Isla Bonita;
Where I'd wish to live with you forever, my senorita.

69
These Moments

In this scenic ambiance, amid Sun's soft radiance,
Let's spend some time, far from sorrow and pain.
Like these swans, we will float on the serene lake;
Perhaps these moments would never come again.

70
Mother

I knocked the door of my house, but you did not open.
My son, why didn't you hear your mother's voice?
At this old age when you abandoned me in hospital;
Perhaps you wanted me never to return my home.

See how shameless your mother is. Still, I came to you;
Maybe these old wrinkled eyes yearned to see the truth.
In bygone days of childhood, on hearing my footsteps;
You used to open the door hastily and snuggled to me.

But now, I felt sad and uncomfortable on seeing that
You were hidden behind the door; waiting for me to go.
I could see your vacillating shadow coming from inside.
Perhaps I knew what was going in your confused mind.

Today I am here to collect the smithereens of old days;
Don't worry my son; Your mother will never come again.
Children change color; mother always remains the same.
Be happy; I will always embrace you if you face any pain.

71
Mother Earth

In the lap of mother earth, feel the eternal bliss,
Embrace the divine life, enjoy the nature's kiss.
As compassionate mother feeds the hungry child,
Benevolent Earth fulfills the need of humankind.
Amid melodies of air let's bask in surreal nature,
Now it is time to cherish this priceless treasure.
Show respect to bounties that she has bestowed,
Else be ready to reap whatever you have sowed.
Now, you have last chance to correct your way,
For prosperous future, respect the nature today.

72

I Dream For Decent Dwelling

I dream for decent dwelling;
In the deafening cacophony.
In this world serenity is scarce;
And our dream home is a farce.

I know, you may think; why?
But trust my words, I did try.
After spending hours of rush,
I need little rest in a small hut.

I spent many days and nights;
Searching little place of mine.
But in the world run by money;
I received only pain and agony.

Our society is for only wealthy;
And souls like me are unworthy.
My sweet home, built with love;
I craved only this many months.

But at the end, I am at crossroad;
With dried eyes and bag of hope.
Despite many barriers and distress;
I'll not hesitate from dreaming again.

One day my diligence will pay me;
The pleasure of owning a dwelling.
A place adorned with my passion;
and crafted with my imagination.

73
Fame

I entered the tinsel town in search of the fame;
There, I witnessed a hostile world for this dame.
I kept waiting at the gates of renowned studios;
At the end when I failed, I wished for an Amigo.

See! The luck finally showed his grace in my life;
I got friendship of an aspirant with a story as mine.
We both worked hard to get the work and name;
But destiny favored him; he achieved the fame.

It was not unexpected to see him leaving me;
My heart was sobbing but didn't show it to him.
Soon I also got the fame and met him once again;
He was looking devastated as he had lost his fame.

Though I consoled him, I preferred to move ahead;
Back in my car when I visited the old memory lanes.
Why relations lose their sheen in the glitter of fame?
Amid this thirst, we will never get inner happiness;

I asked the driver to turn back my brand new car;
I wanted to help my old mate despite the old scars.
His rise and fall had taught the true lesson of life;
Fame's life is short; we should not make it our life.

74
My Father

I yearn to get the blessed clairvoyance;
To envision my late father's divine image.
Why this inconsolable heart still aches?
And these tearful eyes, often wish to rain.

Perhaps somewhere deep in poor heart;
There is a hope to see him on this earth.
Why am I running away from the truth?
And my soul has no belief in life's sooth;

All I wish to walk down the memory lane;
and pick up the old days and their remains.
When he was alive and close to these eyes;
I never realized how important he is in life.

Now his voice often resonates in my mind;
This father's day I yearn my life to rewind.
Whatever be reality; I get solace in dreams;
Where I see his image flashing before me.

I yearn to get the blessed clairvoyance;
To say sorry to him for my all the mistakes.
The saddest part is, we'll never meet again;
He has gone far, leaving behind me in pain.

O! Lord, give me the extrasensory perception;
I yearn to see again; my father's impression.
Although I know, I may not get clairvoyance;
Still, I nurture the fancies that soothe my pain;

75
The Bride of The Himalayan Tree

Somewhere in the Himalayas, I resided in a village;
Where it was hard to get right groom for marriage.
My horoscope had poor Martian planetary position;
And to fix it, I was married with the Himalayan tree.

Now all started searching a boy for my marriage;
Before that'd happen, my parent departed to heaven.
Since then, my ordeal had been an unending spree;
I remained forever, the bride of the Himalayan tree.

The world was not kind to the orphan girl like me;
Humiliated by all, got peace in the shade of the tree.
Many days, months and the years passed like this;
I remained forever, the bride of the Himalayan tree.

One day I heard that trees were cut to build a dam;
But before I reached there, the tree was about to fall.
I tried to hold its trunk, but that effort was in vain;
And I died beneath as bride of the Himalayan tree.

I opened eyes; I found my dead body next to me;
and a charming prince riding on the white horse.
He held my hand and took me to heavenly abode;
Where I stayed forever with my Himalayan love.

{Note: In India, at some places, girl is married to tree as ritual
before marrying a man to rectify Martian planetary position}

ABOUT MANOJ KRISHNAN

Manoj Krishnan is a software engineer by profession, currently working in the US based MNC in Gurgaon. He had completed his B.E. in Electronics & Communication from ITM Gwalior, M.Tech from BITs Pilani and PGDIT from Symbiosis.

He is the author of novel KANISHKA, His poems have been awarded in various national and international literary forums. He has been chosen as one of the world's 50 Contemporary Poets of 2017. His many poems have been selected and published in national and international Anthologies. His short story "Lucky to meet you" has been published in Anthology "Rehnuma" and short story "The Gift" has been selected for publication in Anthology dedicated to Indian Army.

DHARMAYODDHA
KALKI
AVATAR OF VISHNU
Exhilarating
and
furiously paced.
Millennium Post
KEVIN MISSAL

Estenzic Love
Hrishitaa Paraswani

A kind of Commitment
Pratibha Malav

I killed her
SACHIN JHA

LOVE LEFT UNLOVED
FROM THE ONE THEY LOVED
AASHI GUPTA

NIDA AHMED
We Decided on Forever
Based on real life events.

AbstracTales
BY
ANIRUDDHA PATHAK
ANKITA RATHOUR
KRITIKA SHARMA
PALLAVI SAREEN

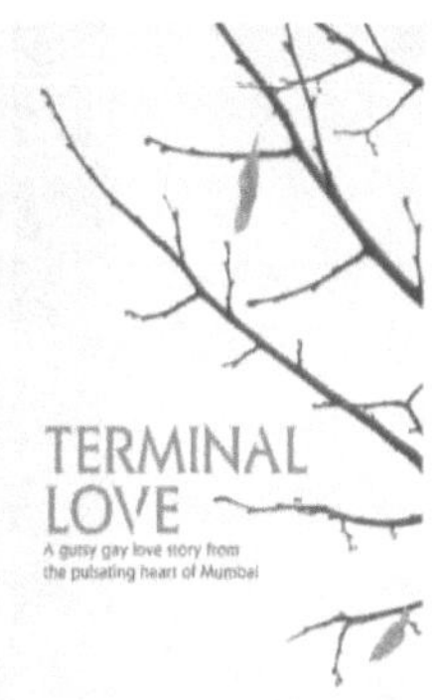

TERMINAL LOVE
A gutsy gay love story from
the pulsating heart of Mumbai
Vicky Arora

The Lady in Me
Banaja Prakashlal Samantaray
Shelo Aura

मैं
और
ये
ज़िन्दगी
संदीप दहिया

स्याही के अक्षर
अनीर

World's First Insta Read
BY
KEVIN MISSAL
KARMA

from the author of
Khan vs Kahn vs Kanh & These Were the Days
Marriage
made in
Mumbai Local
N. S. Ravi

(Wonderfully Broken Series)

www.ingramcontent.com/pod-product-compliance
Lightning Source LLC
LaVergne TN
LVHW040159180726

843489LV00007B/2591